SHORT TALES
Furlock & Muttson Mysteries

THE CASE OF
THE GRUMPY CHICKEN

by Robin Koontz

magic
wagon

visit us at www.abdopublishing.com

Published by Magic Wagon, a division of the ABDO Group, 8000 West 78th Street, Edina, Minnesota, 55439. Copyright © 2010 by Abdo Consulting Group, Inc. International copyrights reserved in all countries.

Short Tales ™ is a trademark and logo of Magic Wagon.

Printed in the United States of America, North Mankato, Minnesota.
092009
012010

 PRINTED ON RECYCLED PAPER

Written and illustrated by Robin Koontz
Edited by Stephanie Hedlund and Rochelle Baltzer
Interior Layout by Kristen Fitzner Denton
Book Design and Packaging by Shannon Eric Denton

Library of Congress Cataloging-in-Publication Data

Koontz, Robin Michal.
  The case of the grumpy chicken / written and illustrated by Robin Koontz.
    p. cm. -- (Short tales. Furlock & Muttson mysteries)
  ISBN 978-1-60270-559-3
  [1. Farm life--Fiction. 2. Birthdays--Fiction. 3. Mystery and detective stories.] I. Title.
  PZ7.K83574Casg 2010
  [E]--dc22
                                        2008032523

"Good morning, Muttson!" said Furlock.
"Do we have any mail?"
"There is a catalog of tuna fish candy," said
Muttson.
"Yum!" said Furlock.
"Yuck!" said Muttson.

"There is also a special delivery letter for you," said Muttson. "It smells like it is from your cousin Buddy."
"Muttson, you have such a good nose!" said Furlock.

Furlock opened the letter.
"You are right. It is from Cousin Buddy," she said. "He wants us to come to his farm right away!"
"I will fire up the Furlock-Mobile," said Muttson.

Soon, they arrived at Buddy's farm.
"Look, my prize cow has letters painted on her!"
Buddy cried.
The cow mooed.
"H DAY," Muttson said to his pocket.

"Why are you talking to your pocket?"
Furlock asked.
"It is my new recording device," said Muttson.
"It writes whatever I say to it."
"You have too many toys," said Furlock.

Buddy led them to the chicken coop.
"Look at Matilda, my prize chicken," said Buddy.
"She will not leave her nest!"
He tossed some corn, but Matilda did not move.

"She always leaps off her nest if I toss corn," Buddy said.

Matilda winked at them.

"Interesting," said Furlock.

"Grumpy chicken," Muttson said to his pocket.

Buddy led them to the sheep pen.
"Look at my prize sheep," he said.
Three sheep had purple letters on them.

"Very interesting," said Furlock.
The sheep baaed.
"P PY BIRT," Muttson said to his pocket.

Furlock looked at the ground.
"Aha!" she cried. "Purple spots in the grass!"
They followed the purple spots to the pigpen.

"Oh no! Look at my prize pig!" cried Buddy.
"HA," Muttson said to his pocket.
"What is so funny?" Furlock asked.
The pig oinked.

"We need more clues," Furlock said.
She licked the H on the pig.
"Yuck!" cried Muttson. "You just licked a pig!"

"It is very sweet," Furlock said.
The animals began licking each other.

Furlock sniffed the air.

"I smell something cooking," she said.

"I do not cook," said Buddy. "I only eat grape jelly sandwiches."

Buddy added, "And my grape jelly is all gone!"

"Aha!" cried Furlock. "I think I know what is going on."
"What is going on?" Buddy asked.

"Aliens," said Furlock.

"Aliens! What do they want?" Buddy cried.

"The aliens gave you a message in secret code," said Furlock.

"They wrote it on the cow, the sheep, and the pig."
Furlock licked her lips.
"They wrote with grape jelly!" she declared.

"What about the smell?" Buddy asked.
"The cooking smell came from their spaceship,"
Furlock said.
She pointed at Matilda.

"And, they traded your prize chicken with a grumpy spy," Furlock said.
Matilda hissed at Furlock.
"Oh dear!" cried Buddy.

Muttson pulled out his recording device.
He scrolled through the pages.
"I think I can read the secret code," Muttson said.
"What is the message?" asked Furlock.

"The letters were HDAY P PY BIRT HA,"
said Muttson. "They spell HAPPY BIRTHDAY!"
"Today is my birthday!" said Buddy. "How did
the aliens know it is my birthday?"

"Follow me," said Muttson.
They followed Muttson to Buddy's house.
"Happy birthday!" said Buddy's mom.
"Mom!" cried Buddy. "When did you get here?"

"I got here while you were in town," said
Buddy's mom.
"I made you a grape jelly cake!"
"That explains the cooking smell," said Muttson.
"And I bet you wrote the birthday message on
the animals."

"That was fun!" Buddy's mom said.
"I like to surprise my son."
"But, what about the grumpy chicken?"
Furlock asked.

"Oh, that silly chicken," said Buddy's mom.
"She is protecting Buddy's birthday
present in her nest!"
The group raced to Matilda's nest.

Buddy's mom tossed a piece of cake on the floor.
Matilda leaped off her nest.
"I knew cake would make her happy,"
Buddy's mom said.

A can of tuna fish was inside the nest.
"Mom, you always surprise me on my
birthday!" said Buddy.
"You need to eat better," said Buddy's mom.
"Eating sounds good," said Furlock.

Muttson's pocket buzzed.

"We must go back to the office," said Muttson.

"Another case has come in."

"Have a piece of grape jelly cake," said Buddy's mom.

"Thank you," said Furlock and Muttson.
"Thank you," said Buddy.
"Muththon, on thoo thuh neth caseth!"
Furlock said.
"I am right behind you," said Muttson.

They jumped into the Furlock-Mobile
and sped away.